THE PUZZLE CLUB™
EASTER ADVENTURE

Adapted by Dandi Daley Mackall

Based on *The Puzzle Club Easter Adventure* original story by Mark Young for Lutheran Hour Ministries

Lutheran Hour
Ministries

CPH
SAINT LOUIS

J
F
Mac

Puzzle Club*™ *Mysteries
The Puzzle Club Christmas Mystery
The Puzzle Club Mystery of Great Price
The Puzzle Club Case of the Kidnapped Kid
The Puzzle Club Poison-Pen Mystery
The Puzzle Club Musical Mystery
The Puzzle Club Easter Adventure
The Puzzle Club Meets The Jigsaw Kids

Cover illustration by Mike Young Productions

Copyright © 1999 International Lutheran Laymen's League
™ Trademark of International Lutheran Laymen's League

Published by Concordia Publishing House
3558 S. Jefferson Avenue, St. Louis, MO 63118-3968
Manufactured in the United States of America

1 2 3 4 5 6 7 8 9 10   08 07 06 05 04 03 02 01 00 99

Contents

Case #99

In the city of New Bristol, spring announced itself with flowers and Easter decorations on every corner. But down at the marina, dark, threatening clouds hid the morning sun. Wild waves crashed the shore, and the smell of fish and the salty sea hung in the air.

By the old lighthouse, a suspicious-looking character lurked in the shadows. "Psst ... here!" he said in a low, gravelly voice.

A large man with a long, scraggly beard and a sea captain's hat cautiously approached the lighthouse. "That you, Sunny Jim?" he whispered.

The shadowy figure remained hidden. "Who else would it be? Cut the chatter,

Captain Moody," the man snarled. "Have you got the goods?"

Captain Moody held out a brown leather briefcase. "All here," he said. "And won't the Greek government be surprised when it finds all its precious Roman coins missing!"

"Speaking of surprises!" shouted the shadowy figure by the lighthouse, his voice no longer gravelly. The man stepped away from the shadow of the lighthouse and into the light. It was none other than Tobias, the Puzzle Club's chief advisor!

"Stolen Roman coins, eh?" Tobias asked. "Well, Captain Moody, your *Roman* days are over!"

Captain Moody threw the briefcase at Tobias and fled in the opposite direction. The case popped open, sending hundreds of gold coins clattering and clanging onto the stone walkway.

Tobias took a deep breath and whistled through his fingers. Two short blasts and one long—the Puzzle Club secret signal. Then he took off running after the thief. "Now, Puzzle Club!" Tobias hollered.

From high above, a rope net dropped from the lighthouse and landed directly over the unsuspecting Captain Moody. "Hey!" shouted the captain, struggling to get free of the ropes. "Help!"

"We've got him!" Christopher shouted down from the top of the lighthouse. He and Korina had been lying in wait to spring their trap.

"We captured the captain!" shouted Korina. "Let's climb down, Christopher."

"I've got a better idea," said Christopher, grabbing one of the ropes that hung over the side of the lighthouse. Hanging onto the rope, he used the side of the lighthouse to rappel down like a mountain climber.

Korina took the other rope and did the same thing. "Hold him, Tobias!" she yelled, thrusting herself down the side of the lighthouse. "We'll be right there!"

Tobias grabbed Captain Moody by the collar and hoisted him out of the rope net. Christopher, then Korina, dropped to the ground in front of Tobias and the captive captain.

"Good work, Puzzle Club!" called Sheriff Grimaldi. He was leading another prisoner who was already captured and handcuffed. The sheriff tugged at the burly prisoner, pulling him into line. "Sorry I was a bit late," said the sheriff. "Sunny Jim was resisting arrest."

The real Sunny Jim, Captain Moody's partner in crime, jerked at his handcuffs. But he didn't stand a chance against the sheriff.

"Another mystery solved, eh Christopher and Korina?" asked Sheriff Grimaldi, wiping his brow. He glanced up and down the docks. "Where's Alex?"

"Alex?" asked Korina. "It was his turn to guard Puzzle Club headquarters." She checked her watch. "Therefore, it is safe to assume that Alex is, at this moment, sitting in headquarters feeling sorry for himself for missing the capture."

"All the same," said the sheriff, "nice work, Puzzle Club. One more case closed."

"Yes, indeed," said Korina. "Puzzle Club Case #99! We can call it *The Case of the Lighthouse Smugglers.*"

"How in the world did you know about us?" asked Captain Moody as Sheriff Grimaldi snapped handcuffs over the captain's chubby wrists.

"We've known about your smuggling ring for weeks," Christopher answered. He gazed all the way up to the bright beam at the top of the lighthouse. "We thought Sunny Jim was using the lighthouse light to signal you, Captain Moody," he said.

Korina grinned at Tobias. "But we could not have solved the mystery without Tobias," she said.

"You can say that again," said Christopher. "Tobias translated your secret signals."

Tobias' faced turned red. He chuckled. "It was just a good thing I knew Morse code, that's all," he said.

"So it's your fault!" Captain Moody snarled at Tobias like a pit bull. "I'll get you for this, Tobias!"

Tobias didn't look a bit worried. "Well, maybe 20 years in jail will cool you off," he said, reaching up and tugging Captain Moody's cap down over his eyes.

Korina watched as Sheriff Grimaldi escorted Captain Moody and Sunny Jim to the police van. "You were great, Tobias," she said. "What would we ever do without you?" She stood on her tiptoes and kissed Tobias' cheek.

"Aaww!" Tobias blushed. Then he leaned down and grabbed his leg. "My goodness," he said, holding the calf of his leg. "Maybe I shouldn't have run like that." He tried to take a step, but he wobbled and nearly fell down.

Christopher rushed to help him. "Tobias! Are you all right?" he asked. He tried to support the weight of the older man.

Tobias rubbed his leg. "Hmm ... maybe my doctor should check this out," he said. He stood up straight and smiled, suddenly his old self again. "I'm all right. You two go ahead. I'll meet you back at Puzzleworks."

"Only if you are sure everything is okay, Tobias," Korina said. "You have to promise to take it slow and easy. You scared me for a minute. Are you positive that you are all right?"

"You two run along," Tobias said. "I'm just fine."

Christopher tossed Korina's bike helmet to her, then pulled on his own. "Maybe you should take the day off, Tobias," he suggested. "I guess you're right though. We had better get back to Puzzle Club headquarters. Alex wasn't too happy about staying behind. It's too bad he had to miss out on all the action."

Korina sighed. "Honestly, Christopher," she said. "It *was* Alex's turn to answer calls at headquarters. He will be just fine."

"I suppose," Christopher said as they mounted their bikes and started back. "Knowing Alex, I'm sure he's keeping himself busy." Christopher gave one last wave to Tobias. "After all, what trouble could he get into at headquarters?"

Stop in the Name of Alex!

Back at Puzzle Club headquarters located above Tobias' puzzle shop, Alex was frustrated. It wasn't fair! Here he was, stuck guarding Puzzle Club headquarters while the rest of the detectives were capturing smugglers.

After all, who had copied the light signals into his notebook? *Alex!* And who had written down every word as Tobias decoded the messages from the lighthouse flashes? *Alex!* But was Alex part of the actual capture? *No!* And why? Because in Korina's records it was his turn to guard headquarters.

Usually Alex loved hanging out at headquarters. One whole part of the attic room housed his costumes. Racks, boxes, and shelves overflowed with enough secret disguises to handle any case.

But today Alex hated being stuck at head-quarters. Korina's experiments lay spread out over a long table under the window. A huge mask, painted to look like a clown seemed to frown at him. Christopher's camera equip-ment covered the far corner of the room.

"*Braawk!*" Sherlock, the Puzzle Club's parakeet mascot, stuck his head out of the clown mask.

"Sherlock!" Alex said, trying to act as if the bird hadn't made him jump. "Watch this."

Alex turned toward the shadowy corner of the attic, where a large figure wearing a trench coat and hat stood perfectly still. "All right, you creepoid!" Alex shouted. "You can't sneak in here past Detective Alex of the Puzzle Club Detective Agency!"

Alex leaped in front of the burglar-shaped figure. Sherlock did a nosedive back inside the mask.

"There's no escape for you!" Alex cried. He reached up and pulled the lightbulb chain. Light splashed over the mannequin he had dressed to look like a burglar. Its plastic body dangled from the clothesline Christopher used to hang photographs to dry.

Alex took another step toward his make-believe intruder. "You forgot about my secret weapon!" he yelled.

Alex flung open his trench coat. A box was strapped across his chest with a leather belt. Alex grabbed the drawstring attached to the side of the box and prepared to pull it.

Suddenly a siren went off. Bells rang and whistles blew. Someone had set off the Puzzle Club security system. Alex forgot about his secret weapon. Heart pounding, he whirled around to face a *real* intruder.

The door to headquarters swung open. A little kid who couldn't have been older than 6 or 7 barged into the room. The boy's brown hair and something about his nose reminded Alex of somebody. It reminded him of Mr. Rafferty, the park maintenance man. This had to be Buzz, Mr. Rafferty's grandson. Alex felt his heart slow down to normal.

Buzz approached Alex as though he didn't hear the alarms he'd set off.

Alex ran over to the keypad and punched in the secret security code to turn off the alarms. "Buzz—" he started.

But Buzz couldn't wait. "Alex! Alex!" he cried. "She's gone! She's missing! You've gotta find her!"

"Oh boy!" said Alex. "A kidnapping!" He whipped out his detective's notebook and pulled his pencil from the top spiral. Wouldn't Korina be jealous when she found out he already was working on a brand-new case!

"Okay, Buzz," Alex said, flipping the pages in his notebook past the Case of the Curious Cobra, the Mystery of Great Price, the Poison-Pen Mystery, and the Musical Mystery until he found a blank page. "Spill it, Buzz. Who was kidnapped? Your sister? Your mother? Your grandmother?"

"My cat!" cried Buzz.

Alex snapped his notebook shut. "You mean cat ... as in *kitty cat*?"

"Yes, Angela," Buzz answered. "She's two years old with light brown fur—"

Alex interrupted. "Wait! Hold it. Time out, Buzz." Alex slid the pencil back into the metal loops. "Look, Buzz, you're a good kid, but The Puzzle Club doesn't find lost pets."

"But Angela's more than a pet." Buzz said it so softly Alex could hardly hear him.

"Listen, Buzz," Alex continued. "If anyone else is ever missing—as in a missing *person*—The Puzzle Club is here to help."

Buzz turned and walked toward the door. "I get it," he muttered. "I guess if you won't help me, I'll just have to do it myself."

As Buzz closed the door to headquarters, Alex remembered his burglar. "Don't think I've forgotten about you!" he yelled, whirling around to face the mannequin.

Alex again prepared to take aim and fire his secret weapon. "Never fear! Alex is here!" he yelled. Then he tugged the string attached to his invention.

The front of the box dropped open to reveal a large spring attached to a mechanical grabber hand. The spiraled wires sprang out of the box, making the hand shoot straight ahead.

"Gotcha now!" Alex warned the dummy. But instead of grabbing the burglar, the mechanical hand smacked the desk and bounced off with a *boing*. Alex's secret weapon flew straight up in the air—straight toward the ceiling fan.

Before he could react, the grabber hand latched on to one of the fan's blades.

"Uh oh," Alex said as he fumbled with his belt, trying to get out of his invention. But there was no time. Alex felt himself being jerked off his feet as the mechanical hand clung to the ceiling fan blade.

"Help!" he screamed as the fan whipped both Alex and his secret weapon around and around in circles. Headquarters and his disguises sailed by in a colorful blur. It was as though Alex were inside a clothes dryer, tumbling like a T-shirt.

Finally, Alex managed to unbuckle his belt. Wiggling and squirming, he broke free from his invention. But he'd forgotten one detail. The box kept spinning in circles. Alex did not. Instead, Alex was flung through the air away from the ceiling fan.

Bang! Crash! Alex slid across the table, sending everything flying—even poor Sherlock! When he came to a stop, Alex felt woozy. The whole room was still swirling, and for a minute he thought he might be sick.

Alex felt for bruises, but except for a slight headache, he was fine. "That was some ride, huh, Sherlock?" he said when his stomach had settled down. He struggled to his feet and grabbed the table for balance.

"*Braawk!*" Sherlock flew to Alex's shoulder and nuzzled his cheek. "*Braawk! Some ride!*" he squawked.

Alex let go of the table and tried to take a step. The room hadn't quite stopped spinning, but at least he could walk.

"I've had enough of guard duty," he said, taking a few more wobbly steps. "This is hard work, Sherlock."

Alex could almost walk like normal again. "Sherlock, let's take a lunch break. How about a pizza?" Alex asked.

"*Braawk! Pizza! Pizza!*" squawked the parakeet. Alex had never known Sherlock to say no to pizza. Alex put his invention back together and strapped it back around his waist.

Alex glanced around headquarters. It looked like a real burglar had been there. The place needed to be cleaned up, but he'd be in better shape to do it after he got some pepperoni pizza under his belt. Besides, he'd done a good job guarding headquarters all morning. Things would be okay until he got back.

"Come on, Sherlock," Alex said. "Headquarters will be all right. What could possibly happen here without us?"

Lean, Mean
Answering Machine

One hour and half a pizza later, Alex and Sherlock made their way back to headquarters. Alex balanced the pizza box containing leftovers on one shoulder and Sherlock on the other.

"I hope Christopher and Korina appreciate all the trouble we went to just to save them each a piece of pizza," he said. "I don't think Korina will notice we ate the pepperoni off her piece, do you, Sherlock?"

"*Braawk! Burp!*" said Sherlock, covering his beak with his wing.

"Real nice, Sherlock. Excuse you!" Alex scolded.

Alex climbed the secret staircase to head-quarters. He put one hand on the doorknob, then remembered to punch in the security code before he opened the door.

To his surprise, Christopher and Korina already were inside. They were standing by the table, hunched over the answering machine.

"Hi, guys!" Alex called, setting down the pizza box. "Sherlock and I are going to clean up the mess we—"

Korina stormed over to him. "Where were you, Alex?" she demanded.

"Well, duh," Alex said, pointing to the word *PIZZA* on the box.

Christopher still was crouched over the answering machine. The red message light blinked on and off. Even though Christopher was 14 and Alex only 11, Alex usually could count on his friend to give him a warm greeting. But this time, Christopher hadn't even looked up.

"What's the matter with you two anyway?" Alex asked, joining Christopher.

"Alex, listen to this." Christopher pressed the *rewind* button on the answering machine.

The tape whirred a long time, then clicked off. Christopher pressed *play.*

A distressed voice came out of the speaker. "Puzzle Club! This is an emergency! Hello? Anyone there?"

There was a pause, a click, and another message: "Please, please Puzzle Club! This is Rafferty! You have to pick up. Something terrible's happened."

"There are a dozen messages just like that one, Alex," Christopher said. He pushed *fast forward,* and the tape whirred ahead. Then he pressed *play.*

If anything, Mr. Rafferty's voice sounded more desperate: "... not there? It's me again— Rafferty. Sorry to keep calling, but I really need your help, Puzzle Club! Please call me!"

Christopher clicked off the answering machine. "Poor Mr. Rafferty," he said, frowning at Alex. "I'd better give him a call." He picked up the phone receiver and dialed.

Korina got nose to nose with Alex. She was 13, and Alex knew she still thought of him as a junior detective, even though Christopher said he wasn't. "You were in charge of headquarters, Alex," she scolded, her hands on her hips. "Why did you leave?"

Alex gulped. He glanced at Sherlock on his shoulder. The bird looked as nervous as Alex felt. "We … uh … we were kinda—"

"*Braawk!*" screeched Sherlock.

Alex was saved from answering by Christopher's shout into the phone. "We'll be right over!" He slammed down the phone and turned to face Korina and Alex. "It's Mr. Rafferty's grandson, Buzz. He's missing!"

The news hit Alex like indigestion. He felt it in the pit of his stomach, as if he'd swallowed a bowling ball. "Not Buzz!" he gasped.

"Poor Buzz," said Korina. "And poor Mr. Rafferty."

Christopher ran to the Puzzle Club headquarters' secret exit. A large club logo—a magnifying glass and a giant eyeball—hid the entrance to a secret chute. Christopher pushed the button on the wall. A circle of glass in the magnifier opened, revealing an escape slide.

"Don't just stand there, Puzzle Club!" yelled Christopher. "Time's wasting!" He jumped through the opening and slid down the chute.

Korina climbed on after him and pushed off down the slide. Alex ran to the opening and caught it just before it closed again. He climbed in and hurtled down after Korina.

Inside the chute, Alex twisted and turned as he zoomed down the slide. Ahead of him he could hear Christopher and Korina clanging and clattering as they wound down the maze of curves.

At the central intersection, tunnels split off in several directions. One led to the alley, one to Puzzleworks, and one to the street. Alex was moving so fast, he almost missed the turn that led to Puzzleworks, Tobias' puzzle shop. He hoped he wouldn't crash into Korina.

"*Braawk!*" Sherlock complained, digging his claws into Alex's shoulder.

"Easy does it, Sherlock!" Alex said. "We're almost there."

Ahead, at the end of the chute, Alex saw the hole open as the door slid back just in time to let Christopher slide through to Puzzleworks. *Plunk! Plunk! Plop!* Christopher, Korina, then Alex landed on their rear ends inside Puzzleworks.

Alex loved Tobias' store. Nobody had more puzzles than Tobias, and their white-haired friend could put anything together. Puzzleworks even smelled like puzzles. It was a mysterious sort of smell—wood and glue mixed with something else he couldn't name.

Tobias was sitting behind the store counter. "Off on another … *pant, pant* … case already, Puzzle Club?" he asked, wheezing.

Alex thought Tobias' face looked red, as if he'd been sunburned.

Tobias put his hands on the counter. "I'll … *pant, pant* … drive you." He started to stand up, then dropped back down into the chair.

Alex, Korina, and Christopher rushed behind the counter and crowded around him. Tobias was breathing hard, like Alex did when he was out of breath from running too fast. But Tobias hadn't been running.

"Tobias?" Alex asked. "What's wrong?"

"Are you okay?" Korina asked and felt Tobias' forehead.

Christopher put his hands on Tobias' shoulders. "Tobias," he said, "sit still, okay?"

Tobias tried to chuckle. "Well, maybe I *had* better rest for a while," he said, taking a deep breath that made him close his eyes. "I'm all right now. Really. You three had better get to your new case."

"We can't leave you, Tobias," Alex said.

"Nonsense," said Tobias, grinning almost like normal. "You three scoot along! Go on now!"

Christopher, Korina, and Alex hesitated, unsure whether to go or stay. Christopher filled Tobias in on Buzz's disappearance, leaving out the part about Alex leaving headquarters and the answering machine unguarded.

"Now go solve that case," Tobias said when Christopher had finished his account. "Poor Rafferty adores that grandson of his. You can't let him down, Puzzle Club."

Christopher, Korina, and Alex biked in silence past the town square. Easter decorations covered the park. Brightly colored Easter eggs hung from several trees. Everywhere, flowers bloomed. But Alex's mind kept drifting back to Tobias.

"Speed it up, Alex!" called Korina from almost a block ahead. "The sooner we end this case, the sooner we can get back and check on Tobias."

Dollars to Donuts

Mr. Rafferty was pacing on his front porch when The Puzzle Club biked up on his lawn. They parked their bikes against a giant cottonwood tree that was just starting to bud. The sun shone through the tree branches, making crooked black lines across the green grass.

Alex lagged behind and let Korina and Christopher walk ahead of him up the sidewalk to the porch. Mr. Rafferty's house was a little smaller than Alex's. The porch sagged in the middle, making it look a little bit like a wooden bridge. Alex wanted to turn and run away, but he knew he couldn't.

"You made it!" cried Mr. Rafferty. He came to the edge of the porch to greet The Puzzle Club. He looked much older and more wrinkled than he had when Alex had seen him a couple days earlier. He was wearing the hat he always had on when he cared for the lawn and flowers in the town square.

Mr. Rafferty studied something he held in both hands. As The Puzzle Club stepped onto the porch, Alex could see that it was a photograph in a shiny, brass frame. But so much light was reflecting off the frame, Alex could not make out who was in the picture.

"Look at this," said Mr. Rafferty, holding the picture out to The Puzzle Club. His gaze never left the face smiling out of the frame. It was as though Mr. Rafferty were hypnotized by it. His voice cracked and he had to look away, but not before Alex saw the tears swimming in his eyes. "That's Buzz with his cat, Angela."

The Puzzle Club closed in for a better look. In the photo, Buzz seemed so happy, a whole lot happier than he'd looked the last time Alex had seen him.

The sight of Buzz's freckled face made Alex feel like crying. He looked away, just as Mr. Rafferty had, and fumbled with his detective's notebook.

"Angela's been missing for two weeks now," Mr. Rafferty explained. He took the picture back and clutched it to his heart.

"Alex?" Mr. Rafferty nudged him with his elbow. "You know my grandson, don't you, Alex?"

Alex cleared his throat. "Yeah, we know each other," he said softly, not looking up at Mr. Rafferty. He pulled the pencil out of the wire spiral at the top of his notebook. Then he acted like he was taking notes. Usually Alex could think of all kinds of notes to write down, but not this time. He just scribbled on the paper: *Buzz.*

Mr. Rafferty held the photo at arm's length, practically shoving it in Alex's face. Alex made himself look at it again. There was little Buzz hugging his cat.

"This morning Buzz took off looking for Angela all by himself," Mr. Rafferty said, a note of pride mixed with the fear in his voice. He sighed. "Buzz sure loves that cat. Got her from the animal shelter—picked her out himself."

Alex let his notebook drop to his side. Buzz had tried to tell him how important his cat was to him. Why hadn't he listened?

"*Braawk!*" Sherlock zoomed in for a better look, then exchanged guilty looks with Alex.

"Angela's picky about the food she eats, you see," said Mr. Rafferty. "That cat only likes to eat fish—nothing but fish. I used to tell Buzz that his cat was going to turn into a fish herself if she wasn't careful."

Christopher put a hand on the man's arm. "We'll take the case, Mr. Rafferty. We'll find Buzz—*and* Angela."

Christopher began pacing the porch. He scratched his head and squinted in concentration. "First, we'll try and follow the same route Buzz took to find Angela," Christopher said. "Then we might be able to find Buzz."

Mr. Rafferty's face lit up like a lightbulb. His shoulders straightened, and he looked a foot taller. "Dollars to donuts that'll work!" he said, taking off his cap and slapping it against his knee. "I knew I was doing the right thing by calling The Puzzle Club."

"You can count on The Puzzle Club, Mr. Rafferty," Korina said. She was examining the porch railing through her magnifying glass.

Christopher peered over Alex's shoulder to glance at his notebook. But Alex didn't have any real notes except for the one word: *Buzz.*

Christopher continued in a voice filled with confidence while Mr. Rafferty seemed to hang on every word. "First stop: the New Bristol Animal Shelter," Christopher announced. "If that's where Angela came from, and that's where Buzz and Angela first met, maybe that's where she *and* Buzz went first."

Somehow the photograph of Buzz and Angela had ended up in Alex's hands. He stared at the little boy hugging his cat. He wished he could do it all over again. He would promise Buzz that The Puzzle Club would find Angela. He knew that's what Christopher would have done. And that's what Tobias would have done too.

Alex didn't see Mr. Rafferty staring over his shoulder at the picture until the older man cleared his throat. "Find my grandson, Alex," he said. "Please find him!"

Alex stared up at Mr. Rafferty. The man's eyes looked like a bigger version of Buzz's eyes.

"I know I can count on you and the rest of The Puzzle Club to find my grandson," said Mr. Rafferty. "I just know it."

Alex felt his face flush. He felt so guilty about turning Buzz away that he couldn't even look at Buzz's grandfather. Instead, he stared at the almost blank page in his detective's notebook.

Alex knew he should say something—anything—to make Mr. Rafferty feel better. But he felt too bad himself to come up with anything good to say.

"You coming, Alex?" Christopher called. He already was straddling his bike, strapping on his helmet.

Alex turned and ran toward his own bike. "Let's get going!" he hollered. He'd do whatever it took to find Buzz and Angela—no matter where he had to go to do it.

"*Braawk! Get going!*" squawked Sherlock, hopping first to Alex's handlebars, then onto his shoulder.

Alex kept pace as The Puzzle Club biked back through New Bristol. Korina and Christopher exchanged a few words, but Alex didn't pay any attention to what they said. He was too busy mentally replaying the dozen frantic messages Mr. Rafferty had left on the answering machine. Over and over he heard Mr. Rafferty's desperate pleas for help.

But that wasn't all that Alex heard replayed in his mind. Buzz Rafferty's voice begging him to find Angela repeated over and over too. But the worst thing he heard was his own voice saying: *"The Puzzle Club doesn't find lost pets."*

Suddenly something caught his eye as they biked past the park. He screeched to a stop. So did Korina and Christopher. On the other side of the street, red lights flashed on and off. Alex squinted to see better. It was an ambulance! And it was pulled up to the curb in front of Tobias' store!

5

Easter Emergency

For a minute Alex couldn't move. As if hypnotized, he watched the red light on top of the ambulance rotate, lighting up Puzzleworks in blood-red flashes.

Beside him, he heard Korina gasp. "Something's happened!" she squealed in a voice he'd never heard her use. Her scream was like fingernails scratching on a blackboard. It sent chills racing up and down his spine. It also brought him out of his shock.

At full speed, Alex pedaled toward Tobias' store with Korina and Christopher following right behind him.

When The Puzzle Club reached Puzzleworks, Alex jumped off of his bike and let it crash to the sidewalk. Then he charged past the gleaming white ambulance. Its doors were flung wide open, as if the paramedics had been in too big of a hurry to close them.

Everything looked blurry to Alex. Whether it was from tears or fear, he didn't know. Someone behind him may have shouted something at him, but he kept going.

At the entrance to Puzzleworks, Alex nearly rammed into one of the paramedics. The man grunted as he backed through the doorway pulling a stretcher on wheels.

Alex couldn't see around the paramedic, but he didn't need to. He already knew who was lying on that stretcher. "Tobias!" he cried. The name felt as though it were ripped from his lungs.

Behind him, Christopher gasped.

"Oooooh!" Korina cried. "Tobias! We never should have left."

The three of them pressed around the stretcher and stared down at their friend. Never had Tobias looked older. His face was as red as if he'd been badly sunburned. He had a plastic mask over his mouth. A tube ran from the mask to a machine held by a second paramedic. Alex felt tears pushing up from deep inside himself.

Tobias smiled weakly at them, then winced. "Don't worry," he whispered, his voice sounding hoarse. "I couldn't get my breath ... so I called 911."

"This is awful!" Alex moaned. "It's all our fault! Korina's right. We never should have left you alone."

"Tobias," Christopher said, nudging in next to Alex. "I'm so sorry."

Korina elbowed her way between them. "We didn't know you were so sick, Tobias," she said, her voice shaky.

"Settle down now," Tobias said. He took several short breaths. "If anyone's to blame, it's me. When I called the doctor earlier today about my leg, she told me to check into the hospital. So ... at least ... now I'm going." He wheezed again. "Maybe those doctors can fix this 'thick head' of mine while I'm there."

Christopher leaned close to Tobias' pillow. "Is it ... is it serious?" he asked, his voice catching.

Alex always thought of Christopher as the strong one, but now he didn't look so strong. Christopher wiped away tears with the back of his hand. Alex knew that when Christopher was just a little kid, his father had died. Tobias had been like a father, or grandfather, to all of them.

Tobias managed to smile up at Christopher. "I won't lie to you, Christopher. It could be very serious," he said.

Tobias took several more short breaths. It seemed to take all the strength he had. "The doc thinks there is a blood clot in my leg. She says it happens a lot with folks my age." Tobias winced again.

Suddenly there were so many things Alex wanted to tell Tobias. He opened his mouth, but the words got stuck in his dry throat.

Even Sherlock didn't make a sound. He just sat quietly on Tobias' pillow as the paramedics began moving the stretcher toward the ambulance.

"I don't understand," Christopher said, walking beside Tobias. "You said you were okay when we left."

"I thought I was okay ... then," Tobias answered. "When I talked to the doctor, she said it wasn't life-threatening unless the clot moved into my lungs."

Tobias coughed several times and took more shallow breaths. Each movement seemed to hurt.

Alex found himself breathing in short breaths, just like Tobias. Seeing his friend in so much pain was worse than anything—much worse than being left out of a case.

"But, Tobias," Korina said, walking alongside the other side of the stretcher. "You have all this difficulty breathing. Does that mean …" She didn't seem able to finish her sentence. Alex had never seen her look so helpless. Korina was always the one with all the answers. Not now. Now all Korina had was one big, hard question—the same one he had. And she couldn't get it out either.

As the paramedics steadied the stretcher on the sidewalk, Alex took Korina's hand. Without taking her eyes off Tobias, she gave Alex's hand a squeeze.

"Tobias, does all your difficulty breathing mean that …" Korina tried again. "Does it mean …"

The paramedics started to lift the stretcher into the ambulance, but Tobias held up his hand for them to wait.

"It may mean that the blood clot has moved to my lungs," he answered. Tobias wrinkled his nose as if he'd just tasted something yucky, then he managed a wry grin.

"And I always thought of myself as such a young fella!" He tried to chuckle but wound up coughing.

"How can you laugh about it, Tobias?" Christopher asked.

Alex was thinking exactly the same thing. There was nothing to laugh about. It was all he could do not to burst out crying right there in front of everybody. "C-c-could you d-d-die?" Alex asked weakly.

For a second Tobias didn't answer. Then his face lit up with a full-watt Tobias grin. "Could I die?" he repeated. "Well, I suppose I could, Alex. I won't lie to you now. But we will all die sometime, you know."

Korina's eyes widened. "B-b-but aren't you afraid?" she asked.

Tobias seemed to think that one over. "Well, I guess I am ... a little. I think everyone would be at least a little afraid," he said. "But it's okay. I can face this."

Alex didn't get it. None of this was making any sense. He'd never thought too much about dying. Right now it sounded pretty scary. "I don't understand, Tobias," he said, fighting tears.

"Listen, Alex," Tobias said with a smile that almost made him glow. "Why should we be so afraid? We know that Jesus is with us. Remember all those times during your cases when you were afraid?"

Alex didn't have any trouble remembering dozens of times he'd been afraid since they had formed The Puzzle Club. He'd been terrified investigating the ghost at Bascomb Mansion. But Tobias had been with them all the way. And when Alex was afraid to sing in the Musical Monster Madness show, it was Tobias who had convinced him that all he had to do was make a joyful noise for the Lord and not worry about all the people watching. Time and time again, in case after case, Tobias had always been there to help.

"I remember, Tobias," Alex said.

"When you were afraid, you came looking for my help, didn't you?" Tobias asked, his gray eyes twinkling.

Tobias glanced at Christopher and Korina. They nodded at him. They'd been scared too. And they'd gone to Tobias for help, just like Alex had.

"That's what it's like with me and the Lord," said Tobias. He pointed across the street toward the park. Colorful Easter eggs hung from the trees. A wooden cross stood in front of the bandshell. Flowers were just starting to poke up from the ground.

"Look around you. All the decorations remind us of Easter and new life." Tobias said. "When Jesus rose from the dead on that first Easter morning, He showed He was God's Son and that even death could not hold Him. When Jesus died to win us forgiveness and rose again on Easter, He made sure that not even death could separate us from God.

"There is no reason to be afraid of anything," Tobias continued. "Jesus will be with me no matter what happens. Whenever you are afraid, remember that God will give you all the strength and courage you'll ever need."

Tobias' stretcher jerked as the crew prepared to lift it up into the ambulance. "I'm sorry, sir," one of the paramedics said to Tobias. "We really can't wait any longer."

Alex's eyes swam with tears as he watched Tobias disappear inside the ambulance. When the heavy white doors slammed shut, his heart leaped in his chest.

Korina squeezed in between Alex and Christopher. Together they pressed their noses to the window in the ambulance door. And there was Tobias, smiling and waving.

"Hey now, Puzzle Club," Tobias said, his voice barely making it through the glass. "No more moping around. You've got a mystery to solve!"

The ambulance drove off, siren blaring. Alex listened to the whine of the siren grow fainter and fainter. The Puzzle Club detectives watched in silence as the white van disappeared, carrying away their best friend.

Follow That Catbird!

Alex kept staring long after the ambulance was out of sight. He had never felt this helpless in his whole life.

"Now what do we do?" Korina asked.

Christopher sighed and stared across the street at the Easter decorations. "We have to find Buzz," he said, "and fast! The sooner we finish this case, the sooner we can take care of Tobias."

"You're right," said Korina. "Easter is Tobias' favorite time of year, and now he's going to miss everything. We have to help him somehow."

Christopher and Korina ran to their bikes and started strapping on their helmets. Alex didn't budge.

"Come on, Alex," Christopher called. "Stop daydreaming."

Alex felt terrible—about Tobias, about Buzz, about the way he'd turned down the case of the missing cat. He'd have to come clean with Christopher and Korina. "Guys, I gotta tell you something ..."

But Christopher and Korina were already on their bikes and waiting at the curb. A florist truck roared by them. The traffic light changed, and a car screeched to a halt. Horns blared.

"You say something, Alex?" Christopher yelled above the street noise.

Alex hopped on his bike, relieved that he didn't have to tell them—not now anyway. Later would be better. "Naw. Never mind!" he shouted, trying to catch up with Christopher and Korina. "Let's find Buzz."

Christopher and Korina broke all speed records getting to the New Bristol Animal Shelter. Alex and Sherlock weren't far behind. The Puzzle Club hurried inside together.

The cluttered animal shelter smelled like a barn that had been sprayed with pine cleaner. Along two walls sat cages of animals—everything from mice, snakes, and iguanas to the usual puppies, cats, and birds.

A boy who looked only a couple of years older than Christopher walked up to them. A badge pinned to his shirt read: "Shelter Volunteer."

"Well, let's see what we have here," said the volunteer. He leaned over to study Sherlock. The parakeet was sitting wide-eyed on Alex's shoulder. "Hmmm. A poor homeless parakeet."

The volunteer poked at a tomato sauce stain on Sherlock's belly. "Looks like he's been chowing some serious pizza," he said and laughed.

Sherlock dug his claws into Alex's shoulder and shook. "*Braawk! Squawk!*" His eyes got so big Alex was afraid they'd pop out of his head.

The shelter volunteer pointed toward the cages. "This way, little birdie," he said, holding his finger out for Sherlock to jump on. "The only cage we have is next to a boa constrictor, but he won't bother you much."

44

Sherlock flapped his wings wildly, then wiggled his way under Alex's cap.

Alex felt claws dig into his hair. "No! You've got it wrong!" he announced to the volunteer. "We're not here for the parakeet. We're here for a boy."

The volunteer stopped and turned around. "A boy at the animal shelter? Very funny," he said.

Alex pulled the photo of Buzz and Angela from the front pocket of his trench coat. He was glad he hadn't had time to take off the coat and his invention. Otherwise, he might have forgotten to bring along the picture.

Alex handed the photo to the volunteer. "We're looking for a boy and his cat—this cat," Alex said and pointed to Angela.

"Hmmm," mumbled the shelter volunteer as he studied the photograph. He handed it back to Alex. "Sorry. Haven't seen either of them."

Sherlock came out of his hiding place under Alex's cap and eased back onto his shoulder. The bird wiped his brow with his green feathered wing.

There was nothing more The Puzzle Club could do at the animal shelter, so Sherlock,

Alex, Korina, and Christopher left feeling defeated. It had seemed like such a great idea.

Halfway down the front steps, Korina said what Alex had been thinking. "Well, that was certainly a dead end."

Christopher stopped on the top step. "Hey, don't give up so easily," he said. He stroked his chin, just like Tobias always did when he was concentrating. "I've got lots of other ideas."

He frowned, stopped stroking his chin, and stared down at Korina and Alex. "Okay, think!" he commanded. "If you were a cat, where would you go?"

Hmmm, Alex thought. *Where would I go?*

"That's it!" Alex exclaimed, snapping his fingers. He dropped to his hands and knees and meowed like a cat.

"*Braawk?*" Sherlock flapped onto Alex's back for a free ride while Alex crawled around and meowed.

Korina shook her head at Christopher. "Sad, isn't it, Christopher," she said. "I just don't think Alex is cut out for detective work."

Alex stopped meowing but stayed down on all fours. "I am too! To figure out where

Angela went, maybe we should act like her—*meow!*—act like a cat!"

Korina crossed her arms and raised her eyebrows at Alex. "That is without a doubt the most unscientific, ridiculous—"

"Brilliant idea, Alex!" interrupted Christopher. He dropped to his hands and knees and crawled around just like Alex. "Come on, Korina!" he shouted. "Give it a—*meow!*—try."

"But … it won't …" Korina sighed, as if giving up. "Oh, all right. But there is no way I'm chasing any mice!"

Korina looked over her shoulders, then eased herself to her hands and knees. "*Meow?*" she said softly, sounding more like a squeaky mouse than a cat.

Alex liked having the whole Puzzle Club team follow his lead. Well, almost all of them. He missed Tobias. He thought of his friend in the hospital and asked God to keep him safe while they looked for Buzz.

Then Alex turned to Sherlock. The parakeet was perched on his shoulder. "Sherlock? Are you a—*meow!*—member of this team or not?"

Sherlock seemed to think that over. Then he raised his beak and started meowing too. "*Braawk! Meow!*" Alex thought Sherlock's version of a cat sounded a lot better than Korina's.

Sherlock flew off Alex's shoulder and hopped around on the ground, meowing like the rest of The Puzzle Club. After a minute, he stopped, lifted his beak, closed his eyes, and sniffed.

Alex smelled it too—something strong, something weird, something stinky.

Sherlock frowned, gagged, and shivered. "*Braawk!*" He opened his eyes and did a double take. Then he stuck out his wing and pointed. "*Braawk! Braawk! Braawk!*" he squawked.

Alex stopped meowing and looked where Sherlock was pointing. The bird took off toward the alley beside the animal shelter. Several garbage cans overflowing with gross, smelly garbage lined the alley.

Korina and Christopher stopped meowing too.

"What's up, Alex?" Christopher asked.

"Come on, Puzzle Club!" shouted Alex. "I think Sherlock's on to something!"

To the Dump, To the Dump, To the Dumb, Dumb Dump

"I still don't get it," Korina said as they stood with Sherlock, staring at a can of smelly garbage next to the animal shelter.

"Think about it, Korina," said Christopher. "Cats love garbage, right?"

"Right," Korina agreed.

"So where would you go to find tons of garbage?" Christopher asked.

"To the dump!" Alex answered. It made sense. And cats could smell stuff great. Angela wouldn't have had any trouble following her nose.

"Good thinking, Sherlock!" Christopher said. "I mean, good sniffing!"

Sherlock leaned against the trash can and puffed out his feathered chest. He looked so proud of himself that Alex had to laugh. Maybe Sherlock would be the one to solve this Puzzle Club mystery. It sure wouldn't be the first time that he had come up with a clue at just the right moment.

"To the dump! To the dump! To the city dump!" cried Alex. And he took off running full speed ahead.

Minutes later, the Puzzle Club detectives were walking through piles of smelly garbage at the New Bristol City Dump. The stench of rotten junk and sour garbage made Alex sick to his stomach. He held his nose and called, "Here kitty, kitty!"

Beside him, Korina and Christopher were calling too. "Here kitty! Here Angela! Buzz, are you here?" they echoed.

Something rattled, then crashed. The Puzzle Club froze. Alex clutched the photograph of Buzz and Angela to his heart.

With Christopher in the lead, they peeked through a pile of old bricks and lumber to see what had made the awful noise. Alex tried to peer around Christopher.

"It's Mr. Craymore," said Christopher. "He's the garbage collector."

Christopher seemed to relax. He pushed his way through the garbage heap to get to Mr. Craymore. The man was unloading trash cans from the back of his truck.

Alex watched in awe as the wiry man hoisted huge metal trash cans as if they were pillows. He was bone-thin, but he dumped each huge can of garbage onto a stinking mountain of junk.

Alex didn't feel relieved at all to see Mr. Craymore. "That guy gives me the creeps," he whispered.

Korina gave Alex her know-it-all look. "Yes, Alex. But we are on a case, and he might have a clue," she said.

Korina grabbed the photo from Alex's hands. Then, waving it in her hand, she ran ahead of Christopher. "Hello there," she called. "Mr. Craymore?"

Mr. Craymore turned and frowned at Korina.

Korina walked right up to the man and held out the picture. "Have you seen this boy or his cat?" she asked.

Still frowning, Mr. Craymore took the picture from Korina. He adjusted his glasses and squinted through thick lenses at the photograph. "Nope," he said. "Ain't seen this boy around here. No way. No how. And as for that cat, do you know how many cats I see in a day, Missy?"

Mr. Craymore shook his head and turned his back on Korina. "Finding a cat and a boy? That's downright hopeless," he muttered under his breath. He stomped off, tossing the picture over his shoulder as he headed toward his truck.

"But, Mr. Craymore—" called Korina, catching the picture before it landed in the garbage.

"And now you've made me late," he hollered. "Leave me alone!" Without turning back, Mr. Craymore climbed into his truck, slammed the door, and drove away.

Korina, Christopher, and Alex stared after the retreating truck.

"Well, he sure got up on the wrong side of the dump this morning, didn't he?" Christopher said, scratching his chin.

"Christopher!" exclaimed Korina, coming to life. "I have an idea." She wheeled around to face Alex. "Alex?"

"What?" Alex asked, wondering if somehow she'd figured out that he was to blame for everything.

Korina grinned at him. "Instead of your idea about *acting* like a cat, let's try it *my* way and *think* like a cat," she suggested.

"Huh?" Alex asked, somewhat confused.

"What's the first thing you think of when I say *cat*?" asked Korina.

Alex hated games like this, and Korina knew it. Why couldn't she say what she meant? He looked to Sherlock for help. "Birds?" he asked.

Sherlock flapped his wings. "*Braawk!*" he called out, then gave Alex a playful *bonk* on the head.

Christopher gave it a try. "The first thing I think of when you say *cat* is *milk*."

Korina grinned even wider. "And flea collars, catnip, rubber mice … Get it?"

Alex and Christopher got it at the same time. "A pet shop!" they shouted.

The Puzzle Club raced back to the animal shelter to get their bikes and head for the pet shop. "Hold on, Buzz and Angela!" shouted Korina. "The Puzzle Club is on the way!"

If Wishes Were Fishes

Korina led the way through the front door of the New Bristol Pet Shop. A little bell rang as Alex shut the door behind them. Alex wished they would find Angela and Buzz waiting in the store. Then he remembered that prayers were a million times better than wishes, so Alex prayed that Buzz—and Angela—would be safe.

The smell of wet fur and mint air freshener reminded Alex of Tobias' Ark, the pet shop Tobias had owned before he opened Puzzleworks. The thought of Tobias lying in a hospital bed made Alex feel like crying again. He bit his lip and prayed silently: *Dear God, please take care of my friend Tobias.*

Christopher and Korina started down the center aisle of the pet shop. Sherlock perched on Alex's shoulder, flapped his wings, and slapped Alex in the cheek.

"Sherlock," Alex protested, "watch what you're—"

"Shhh!" Korina said, her index finger raised to her lips.

Alex could hear something—someone— singing.

"Scrubba-dubba-dub! A stinky poodle in the tub!" sang the voice.

Alex followed the voice to a big tub of bubbles in the back of the shop. A young woman in a uniform with the sleeves rolled up stood singing over the tub. Her arms were elbow-deep in soapsuds. Then Alex saw a big dog snout sticking out of the bubbles.

"Excuse me," Alex said, clearing his throat. He held out the photo of Buzz and Angela.

The woman kept shampooing the dog, so Alex pushed the picture in front of her face. "Have you seen this little boy and his cat?" he asked.

"I'm a dog person," the woman answered in a singsong voice. "Most cats look the same—not like dogs."

As if a real cat had just been stuck in front of him, the dog suddenly sprang out of the soapsuds and lunged toward the picture. Bubbles flew everywhere.

"Bad doggie!" screamed the lady. "*Bad* doggie!"

The dog made a sliding jump to the counter, splashing Christopher, Korina, and Alex. Dogs barked from all over the store. Birds squawked. Cats hissed.

The sudsy poodle made a flying leap to the top of the iguana cage. The woman ran over just in time to catch the escaped poodle as he headed for the snake cage. By the time she grabbed him, her uniform was soaking wet.

"Now," she said, "where was I?" She shook some bubbles off her pants, then turned and scowled at Alex. "Nope. I haven't seen the boy or the cat."

At the mention of *cat,* the wet poodle squirted out of the woman's hands. The chase was on again. "Stop that, you bad doggie!" she screamed.

"I'll grab him!" Alex yelled. He'd just remembered that he still had his hand-grabber invention belted around his waist. Alex opened his trench coat and pulled the string trigger. The box opened, and the hand sprang out. Sherlock squawked and flew to safety.

The poodle slid to a stop at the feet of a customer who was shopping for an Easter rabbit. As Alex's mechanical hand-grabber reached for the poodle, the dog tried to shake soapy water off his fur.

Just in time, the poodle glanced up and spotted the hand headed his way. He dodged it in the nick of time. The mechanical hand missed the dog, but it landed square on the rear end of the unsuspecting customer as he bent over to pick up one of the rabbits.

"Yeow!" wailed the man, straightening up fast, rabbit in hand. The man stumbled backward and toppled into the tub of bubbles.

"Oops," Alex said weakly, tucking the spring arm back into the box. "Sorry about that."

Korina scratched her head and sighed. "Looks like another dead end, Christopher," she said. They mumbled a quick apology to the pet store woman and headed for the door.

Alex couldn't wait to get out of the shop. He hurried down a side aisle, past the goldfish aquarium. A huge goldfish stared bug-eyed at him through the glass.

"Wait a minute," Alex said, stopping mid-stride. He could feel an idea hatching. "Fish! That's it!" He stared into the aquarium and thought hard. "What did Mr. Rafferty say?" he mumbled, trying to remember something Buzz's grandfather had said.

In his head, Alex could picture Mr. Rafferty. But he had to struggle to remember his words. Hadn't he said that Buzz was afraid Angela might starve away from home? He'd said that Angela only liked to eat fish—*nothing but fish.*

"That's it!" Alex screamed, running outside to catch Korina and Christopher. "Fish! Angela loves fish! And where do you find loads of fish besides in a pet store?"

Korina and Christopher grinned at each other, then at Alex. "The marina!"

Alex was out of breath as The Puzzle Club entered the marina. Sherlock had ridden on

Alex's head the whole way, so he wasn't tired at all.

"Wow!" Alex cried, surveying the harbor—the lighthouse, the docks, the boathouses. "Where do we start?"

As usual, Christopher took charge. "Let's split up," he told Korina and Alex. "Sherlock, fly up and have a look around."

Sherlock did as instructed, saluting Christopher before spreading his wings and soaring over the waters.

Korina whipped out her biggest magnifying glass and stared through it, handing Alex her small magnifier.

"Good," Christopher said. "You two start at opposite ends of the marina. I'll search the middle."

The Puzzle Club split off in different directions. Alex took off down a long, wooden pier. As he walked, he stared through the magnifying glass, looking for clues—cat hairs, bits of clothing, anything.

Alex looked back to see where Christopher and Korina were. Korina was hunched over her magnifier at the end of the far pier. Christopher was tipping up a rowboat that was turned upside down on the shore. He looked under it, then eased it back down.

Alex turned back to his own business and continued down the dock. He peered straight down through the magnifying glass when—*bonk!*—he smashed into something. He looked up into the biggest pair of fish eyes he'd ever seen. A huge, dead tuna hung from a rope, displayed above the docks. It swung back and forth and looked like it was laughing at Alex for being so scared.

"Now that's what I call a fish!" Alex muttered, glad Korina hadn't seen how scared he'd been.

A loud boat horn sounded from somewhere out at sea. Alex turned and spotted a fishing boat tied to the pier. The boat was loaded with enough fish to last Angela through nine lives. "And that's even better," he said, getting to his feet to investigate the boat.

Alex gave the Puzzle Club whistle—two shorts, one long. He wanted Christopher and Korina to be in on the find. Surely Angela would be on that boatload of fish. Alex ran straight for the boat, but he slammed on his brakes when he heard a squeal. *Eeek.*

Alex listened. It might have been a cat squeal. He heard it again. *Eeek.* It was coming—not from the boat of fish—but from a broken-down tugboat tied to the pier. "Angela?" he called, racing for the tug.

The tugboat must have been abandoned there for years. It had rolled almost completely onto its side. Alex could see holes and rotten planks sticking out above the water.

He stopped in front of the tug and listened. Nothing but the squeak of the creaky wood. But if there was even a small possibility that Angela and Buzz were on board, he had to investigate.

Alex started to step onto the tugboat when he heard Christopher and Korina running down the pier toward him.

"Alex!" Christopher shouted. "Don't! Stay off of there!"

"No," Alex shouted back. "It's all my fault. Buzz is missing because of me! He came to the office this morning to get our help to find Angela and I sent him away. Now *I've* gotta find him!"

Alex took a deep breath and jumped off the pier and onto the broken-down tugboat. He heard the *eeek* sound again, but this time it didn't sound at all like a cat. The tugboat rocked and bucked, sloshed and twisted.

Korina gasped. "Alex!" she screamed. "That sound—it's not a cat! It's the boat pulling against the ropes. Quick—get off of there!"

Korina and Christopher ran toward him as Alex tried to balance himself on the rotten planks, straddling a huge hole in the deck. He felt the planks give way under his feet just as he saw Christopher and Korina's outstretched hands. Alex grabbed onto both their hands while the floor beneath him cracked and gave way.

Alex felt himself fall through the hole. Down he went into the murky darkness, pulling Christopher and Korina in after him!

Sink or Swim

Alex, Korina, and Christopher crashed through the broken deck and landed with a huge splash inside the broken-down tugboat. Their screams were swallowed by the water.

Alex came up spouting a mouthful of the cold, fishy sea. He stood up in waist-deep water, scooched his hat back on straight, and tried to catch his breath. Now what had he done? Not only had he fallen through the deck of the tugboat, he had pulled Christopher and Korina down with him.

"Is that you, Alex?" came a faint voice that didn't belong to Korina or Christopher. For a minute, Alex thought he'd imagined it.

Alex turned around, afraid to hope that it could be, might be—

"Buzz!" he cried.

Buzz, soaking wet and shivering, stood not four feet away from Alex.

"I-I-I thought I heard Angela in here," Buzz said and sniffed and wiped at his eyes. "I tried to save her. Then I fell through the deck. And Angela wasn't even in here. And neither was anybody else. And—" Buzz broke down into sobs. "And I've been stuck in this boat for hours!" Buzz buried his face in his hands and cried.

Alex sloshed his way over to Buzz and put one arm around the younger boy. "I'm so sorry, Buzz. I didn't think a missing cat was such a big deal. But it *was* a big deal," Alex said. "You were upset and hurting. And I should have helped you."

Buzz stopped sobbing and looked up at Alex. "It's okay, Alex. You're here now," Buzz said. "All I want to do is get out of here."

Christopher moved to the other side of Buzz. "And that's just what we're going to do, Buzz," Christopher said. "We're going to get you out of here." He banged on the door of the tugboat, but it wouldn't budge.

Alex spotted a round window that was now almost on the ceiling instead of the wall of the tugboat. "Maybe this porthole will open," he said, tugging at the metal latch. But the porthole window wouldn't open.

"I've tried all that," Buzz said, breaking into tears again. "It's no use. It's hopeless."

"No, it isn't, Buzz," Alex said. "Not when Jesus is with us." Alex knew that was exactly what Tobias would say if he were in the boat with them. In fact, he could almost hear his friend's voice.

Korina must have been thinking about Tobias too. She sloshed through the water and stood next to Alex. "Do you think Tobias is still at the hospital?" she asked. "I wonder if—"

The boat shook. Korina gasped and grabbed onto Alex, nearly pushing him under the water.

Outside the roar of a powerboat got closer and closer, then moved farther away. As the noise decreased, the wake the boat had made increased. Waves splashed against the feeble tugboat, sending it into a fit of rocking. Water sloshed inside the tug, splashing the kids as they clung to one another.

"Alex!" cried Buzz. "What are we going to do?"

Alex opened his mouth to speak, and water splashed into it. He coughed and sputtered.

Then he got an idea. "Sherlock!" he said, snapping his fingers. "*He* can help us!"

A huge wave slammed against the tugboat. Christopher lost his balance and fell into Korina. She helped lift him out of the water. "Let's give Sherlock the signal," she said.

Together The Puzzle Club whistled—two shorts, one long. Alex prayed Sherlock could hear it. Then he heard the familiar "*Braawk!*"

Alex pulled his soggy notebook from inside his trench coat and found a mostly dry page. It was the page he'd written *Buzz* on. Alex took out the pencil and scribbled *Help! Marina!* over the whole page just as Sherlock zoomed through the hole in the deck and landed on his shoulder.

"Good boy," Alex said. He ripped out the note and held it up to Sherlock. "Go get help!"

"*Braawk! Help!*" squawked Sherlock as he grabbed the paper from Alex's hand and flew back through the hole.

Buzz and The Puzzle Club cheered as Sherlock flew off. Alex gave high fives to everybody.

Suddenly a loud diesel horn blared. They stopped celebrating and stared wide-eyed at one another.

"Uh oh," Christopher said. "What could that be?"

The blast came again, louder this time, and 10 times bigger than the powerboat's horn. Huge waves knocked the tugboat. This time, instead of sloshing back and forth, the water kept rising. In an instant, cold, dank seawater had risen to Alex's chin.

"We're—gulp—sinking!" yelled Korina.

"I'm going to try something!' Christopher yelled above the roaring engine. He grabbed a metal pole that ran from the floor to the ceiling of the tugboat. Hurling himself out of the water, he tried to climb up. But the pole collapsed, and Christopher came splashing down.

Alex rushed to help, but Christopher disappeared under the rising water. Finally, he struggled up and gasped for air. "I'm okay," he said. "Find something to hold onto."

Korina held onto a metal handle on one wall. Buzz and Alex grabbed onto a wooden box in the corner. But the waters rose higher and higher.

"I'm scared, Alex," Buzz said, crying, as he scooted higher on the box to keep his head out of the water.

Alex was scared too, but he kept hearing Tobias' words. "It will be okay, Buzz," Alex said, surprised that he really did believe what he was saying. "Our friend Tobias told us about trusting in God, especially when things are scary. He said God would give us all the courage we'd need."

Christopher called over to them, "I'd say now seems like a great time to remember that advice. God is right here with us."

It is strange, Alex thought. The waves still splashed, and the water still rose, but somehow the sinking tugboat seemed a little less scary. Alex could feel his head clear. And that's when he got an idea.

"Hey!" he hollered. "I know how to get out of here!"

Alex opened his trench coat and pulled the drawstring on his invention. The box sprang open, and the grabber-hand shot straight up and out. The hand zoomed toward the hole in the deck and clamped itself to the rim of the hole.

"Perfect!" Alex shouted. He unbuckled the belt and held tightly to the box as it slipped off his waist. Then he pulled the box behind a pipe and wedged it in place. It didn't move when he let go. "There!" he announced. Then he wrapped his belt around the pipe and the box to make sure it wouldn't come loose.

Christopher and Korina lifted Buzz onto the spring arm of Alex's invention. They steadied him while he climbed toward the hole and safety.

"Keep going!" Korina shouted, grunting as she pushed with Christopher and helped Buzz inch his way upward.

As Buzz approached the hole, Alex saw him stick his hand up toward daylight as another, bigger hand reached down to pull him up.

"Hurry up down there!" someone called. It was Sheriff Grimaldi! Sherlock must have brought help.

Korina, then Alex, and finally Christopher jumped on the spring arm and crawled toward safety. As soon as Alex stuck his head out of the hole, he saw Sheriff Grimaldi. Sherlock was perched on his shoulder. Mr. Rafferty was lifting Buzz from the tugboat deck to the safety of the pier.

The deck creaked and groaned as Alex tried to pull himself up onto the broken planks. He felt the boards crack around him.

"Quick!" ordered the sheriff. "We're almost out of time!"

Korina was just in front of Alex on the tugboat deck. She wheeled around and grabbed Alex's wrist. Then Korina and Sheriff Grimaldi pulled Alex up and out and onto the deck of the tugboat.

Christopher's head popped up through the hole in the deck, and the sheriff gave him a hand. The tugboat groaned. Water splashed onto the deck and rushed down through the hole.

"It's sinking!" yelled Mr. Rafferty from the pier. He leaned over and reached out a hand for Alex. Alex grabbed the side of the pier and climbed out of the boat with the help of Buzz and his grandfather.

Korina, Christopher, and Sheriff Grimaldi lunged for the pier just as the tugboat dropped still lower. With help, they scrambled to safety as the tugboat gurgled and sank beneath them.

From the docks, everyone watched as the old tugboat disappeared under the sea. As it sank, Alex felt a huge wave of gratitude wash over him.

"Wow!" he said. "That was a close one!"

New Beginnings

Alex silently said a prayer of thanks as bubbles closed over the last bit of the sinking tugboat. He knew Christopher and Korina probably were doing the same thing.

"Oh, Granddaddy," Buzz said, hugging Mr. Rafferty. "I shouldn't have run away. I'm sorry. It's just that I had to look for Angela."

A tear slid down the park maintenance man's cheek as he hugged his grandson. "You're safe now," he said. "That's all that matters. And we'll find your cat, Buzz."

"You bet we will!" Alex said. No case had ever seemed more important to him. He was ready to search for Angela until he saw her safe in Buzz's arms again.

There was only one thing more important to Alex than finding Buzz's cat. Only one thing could keep him from starting his search that very minute.

"If it's okay with you, Buzz," Alex said, petting Sherlock's head with his finger, "there's something really, *really* important we have to do first."

Alex, Korina, and Christopher had raced to the hospital to see Tobias right after escaping from the tugboat. He had looked small and weak in his metal hospital bed. But after a couple of days, Tobias was almost back to his old self again, just as everyone had been praying.

In fact, Tobias had recovered so quickly that the doctor said he could go home early. Alex was glad. He hadn't liked the hospital very much. The nurses never let The Puzzle Club stay long.

Now he and Christopher and Korina were on their way to visit their friend at home. It would have been a perfect day, except for one thing. Even though they'd been looking constantly for her, they still hadn't found Buzz's cat. But The Puzzle Club wasn't about to give up.

As they walked up to Tobias' door, Alex wished he could bottle up the fresh air and bring it to Tobias. The sun shone brightly, and the flowers edging Tobias' lawn bloomed in more colors than Joseph's many-colored robe. In the park across the street, morning dew glistened on the green grass, making the Easter decorations sparkle.

Korina knocked on Tobias' front door.

"Come in," called Tobias. "The door's open."

It was good to hear his cheery voice. Christopher, Korina, Alex, and Sherlock walked through Tobias' living room toward the bedroom in back.

Tobias was sitting up in bed. "What a pleasure to see The Puzzle Club!" he said, grinning.

Buzz and Mr. Rafferty stood at the foot of Tobias' bed. Buzz held an Easter basket filled with candy eggs for Tobias. Mr. Rafferty had ̄ed a pot of yellow and red tulips on the ̄ide table.

"It's great to see you back home, Tobias," Christopher said.

"It's great to be back," Tobias answered. His voice still sounded hoarse and weak. "The doc gave me some medication to clear my lungs. But I'm going to be okay, I just need a few more days of rest."

A knock sounded at the front door. Alex hollered, "Come in! It's open!"

They heard the door open and shut and footsteps cross the living room. Then Mr. Craymore stuck his head inside the bedroom. He still wore his gray uniform and cap. He was carrying a big cardboard box. Squeaky little sounds were coming from the box. "Meow. Mew."

"Angela!" Buzz screamed. He ran to Mr. Craymore, reached inside the box, and pulled out his very own, purring cat. Angela licked Buzz's chin as he buried his face in her soft fur.

Mr. Craymore shifted his weight and cleared his throat. "That ain't all," he said. He knelt to the floor, set the box down, and gently tilted it for everyone to see inside. And there were three little kittens, all meowing.

"Kittens!" Alex exclaimed.

"After your visit, I found the cat and her little ones on my route," Mr. Craymore explained.

Christopher knelt beside Buzz and lifted up one of the kittens. Alex could hear it purr. "So Buzz," Christopher said, petting the small bundle of fur, "Angela was never really missing."

Korina leaned down and picked up a little kitten that looked like a miniature version of Angela. "Angela was just looking for a safe spot to have her babies," she said.

Alex thought about how hard they had looked for Angela. "When I was a cat," he said, "I sure didn't think about having babies."

Sherlock squawked and shrugged his feathers, then flew off Alex's shoulder.

Mr. Craymore stood up and tipped his hat in Tobias' direction. Then he waved a hand at Buzz and Angela. "Be seeing you," he said gruffly and headed out the bedroom door.

Buzz hurried after him. "Mr. Craymore?" he called.

Mr. Craymore stopped and turned back toward Buzz. "Eh?"

"Thanks for taking care of Angela ... and her babies," Buzz said.

Mr. Craymore smiled a toothy grin. Alex couldn't remember seeing anything but a frown on the man's face.

"Well," said Mr. Craymore, turning a little red in the face, "them kittens sure are cute. I mean, for being cats and all."

"Why don't you take one when they're old enough?" Buzz asked. Buzz looked at Angela, who was still curled up against his chest. "I'm sure Angela wants a good home for her babies."

Mr. Craymore's smile widened so much that Alex could see he was missing a couple of teeth.

"You know," Mr. Craymore said slowly, scratching his hair under his hat, "to tell you the truth, I've seen many cats out at the dump, and most of them are wild. Can't get near them wild cats. But a pet? A pet's different. The truth is, I've always kind of wanted a cat of my own."

Mr. Craymore shot a glance at Mr. Rafferty, who smiled his approval. "Yes, sir," said Mr. Craymore, "I'll take one of them cute little kitties. Thank you very much."

The room went quiet for a minute. Even the kittens stopped mewing. Then everybody turned toward Tobias.

Tobias coughed and cleared his throat. "Looks like everything turned out all right. Another mystery solved. Guess you did just fine without me, eh Puzzle Club?" he said.

Christopher walked over to Tobias' bed. "Are you kidding, Tobias?" he asked. "We couldn't have done anything without you."

Tobias wrinkled his forehead. "Me? But I've either been sitting down or stretched out on my back this whole time," he said.

Korina walked to the other side of the bed and fluffed up Tobias' pillow. "Yes, but you've reminded us about Easter and Jesus. And you taught us that God loves us and is always with us, no matter what happens," Korina said.

Tobias' eyebrows shot up, and his eyes grew wide. "You've got it!" he said, his eyes glistening like the dew in the park. "Not only did you listen to what I said, you put those words into action!"

Tobias swallowed and stammered a little, as he usually did when he got emotional. "N-n-now here, P-P-Puzzle Club," he said, pointing to the flowers Mr. Rafferty had brought him. "Go outside and plant these flowers for me, will you? They'll look mighty festive out there. We've all got a lot to celebrate this Easter."

Alex had to agree. They did have a lot to celebrate. Besides celebrating Jesus' resurrection, they would celebrate that Tobias was going to be as good as new. And The Puzzle Club had found Buzz. And Mr. Craymore had found Angela and the bonus surprise of kittens! It was an Easter Alex knew he would never forget.

"We'll plant those flowers, Tobias!" said Korina.

Christopher took the clay flowerpot and started outside. Buzz was close on his heels.

Alex followed them. "Are you coming, Sherlock?" he called. But the parakeet was nowhere in sight.

Alex stopped and turned around to look for the Puzzle Club mascot. Then he spotted him on the floor, his feathers ruffled, surrounded by three little kittens.

"*Braawk! Braawk!*" squawked Sherlock.

The kittens tumbled over each other and closed in on the frightened bird. Sherlock backed into the corner and looked around wide-eyed.

Alex laughed. The sight of big, brave Sherlock, who had survived so many cases, now cornered by three tiny kittens was too funny.

Tobias laughed at the sight so hard that his bed started to shake.

"Take it easy, Sherlock," Alex said and laughed. "Help is on the way."